D0867281

A Note to Parents and Caregivers:

Read-it! Readers are for children who are just starting on the amazing road to reading. These beautiful books support both the acquisition of reading skills and the love of books.

The PURPLE LEVEL presents basic topics and objects using high frequency words and simple language patterns.

The RED LEVEL presents familiar topics using common words and repeating sentence patterns.

The BLUE LEVEL presents new ideas using a larger vocabulary and varied sentence structure.

The YELLOW LEVEL presents more challenging ideas, a broad vocabulary, and wide variety in sentence structure.

The GREEN LEVEL presents more complex ideas, an extended vocabulary range, and expanded language structures.

The ORANGE LEVEL presents a wide range of ideas and concepts using challenging vocabulary and complex language structures.

When sharing a book with your child, read in short stretches, pausing often to talk about the pictures. Have your child turn the pages and point to the pictures and familiar words. And be sure to reread favorite stories or parts of stories.

There is no right or wrong way to share books with children. Find time to read with your child, and pass on the legacy of literacy.

Adria F. Klein, Ph.D.
Professor Emeritus
California State University
San Bernardino, California

Editor: Jill Kalz
Designer: Nathan Gassman
Page Production: Tracy Kaehler
Creative Director: Keith Griffin
Editorial Director: Carol Jones
The illustrations in this book were created digitally.

Picture Window Books
5115 Excelsior Boulevard
Suite 232
Minneapolis, MN 55416
877-845-8392
www.picturewindowbooks.com

Printed in the United States of America.

Library of Congress Cataloging-in-Publication Data
Jones, Christianne C.
Nate the dinosaur / by Christianne C. Jones ; illustrated by Len Epstein.
p. cm. — (Read-it! readers)
Summary: Ever since Uncle Clayton gave Nate a dinosaur costume for his birthday,
Nate has been misbehaving by acting like a dinosaur, and his sister can hardly wait for
her birthday to see what Uncle Clayton brings her.
ISBN 1-4048-1728-X (hardcover)
[1. Costume—Fiction. 2. Behavior—Fiction. 3. Birthdays—Fiction. 4. Uncles—
Fiction.] I. Epstein, Len, ill. II. Title. III. Series.
PZ7.J6823Mac 2005
[E]—dc22
2005027175

Nate the Dinosaur

by Christianne C. Jones
illustrated by Len Epstein

Special thanks to our advisers for their expertise:

Adria F. Klein, Ph.D.
Professor Emeritus, California State University
San Bernardino, California

Susan Kesselring, M.A.
Literacy Educator
Rosemount–Apple Valley–Eagan (Minnesota) School District

PICTURE WINDOW BOOKS
Minneapolis, Minnesota

It all started on Nate's birthday.

Uncle Clayton gave Nate a
dinosaur costume.

After that, Nate thought he
was a dinosaur.

He growled, snorted, stomped, and caused trouble.

He chased our dog around the yard.

He stomped across my city of blocks.

He ripped through all of my dad's newspapers with his claws.

He whipped his tail in circles and broke my mom's dishes.

Mom and Dad didn't know what to do with Nate.

13

It wasn't fair.

Nate got to do whatever he wanted.

But I had a plan.

My birthday was a week later, and I
knew what I wanted.

When Uncle Clayton showed up at my party with a gift, I couldn't wait to open it.

Was it what I asked for?

Yes! It was my very own costume.

If Nate got to be a dinosaur, then I got to be a cat.

I wonder what Mom and Dad
will ask Uncle Clayton for on
their birthdays?

More *Read-it!* Readers

Bright pictures and fun stories help you practice your reading skills. Look for more books at your level.

At the Beach 1-4048-0651-2
Bears on Ice 1-4048-1577-5
The Bossy Rooster 1-4048-0051-4
Dust Bunnies 1-4048-1168-0
Flying with Oliver 1-4048-1583-X
Frog Pajama Party 1-4048-1170-2
Galen's Camera 1-4048-1610-0
Jack's Party 1-4048-0060-3
The Lifeguard 1-4048-1584-8
Mike's Night-light 1-4048-1726-3
The Playground Snake 1-4048-0556-7
Recycled! 1-4048-0068-9
Robin's New Glasses 1-4048-1587-2
The Sassy Monkey 1-4048-0058-1
Tuckerbean 1-4048-1591-0
What's Bugging Pamela? 1-4048-1189-3

Looking for a specific title or level? A complete list of *Read-it!* Readers is available on our Web site:
www.picturewindowbooks.com